Sorry To Hear About Your Fish

By: Colleen Hollis

Illustrated and digitized by Colleen Hollis
Copyright © 2024 Colleen's Children Line Inc. Ltd.
Publisher: Colleen's Novels Inc. Ltd.
ISBN: 978-1-964768-02-1

I am so sorry to have heard about your beloved fish

Many fish live in the same location most of their lives.

So for some people, they see fish as a boring pet and lose interest pretty quickly.

Oftentimes they don't understand the connection that is formed between a kiddo and their finned friends.

People who don't get it could say, "What can you really even do with a fish anyway?"

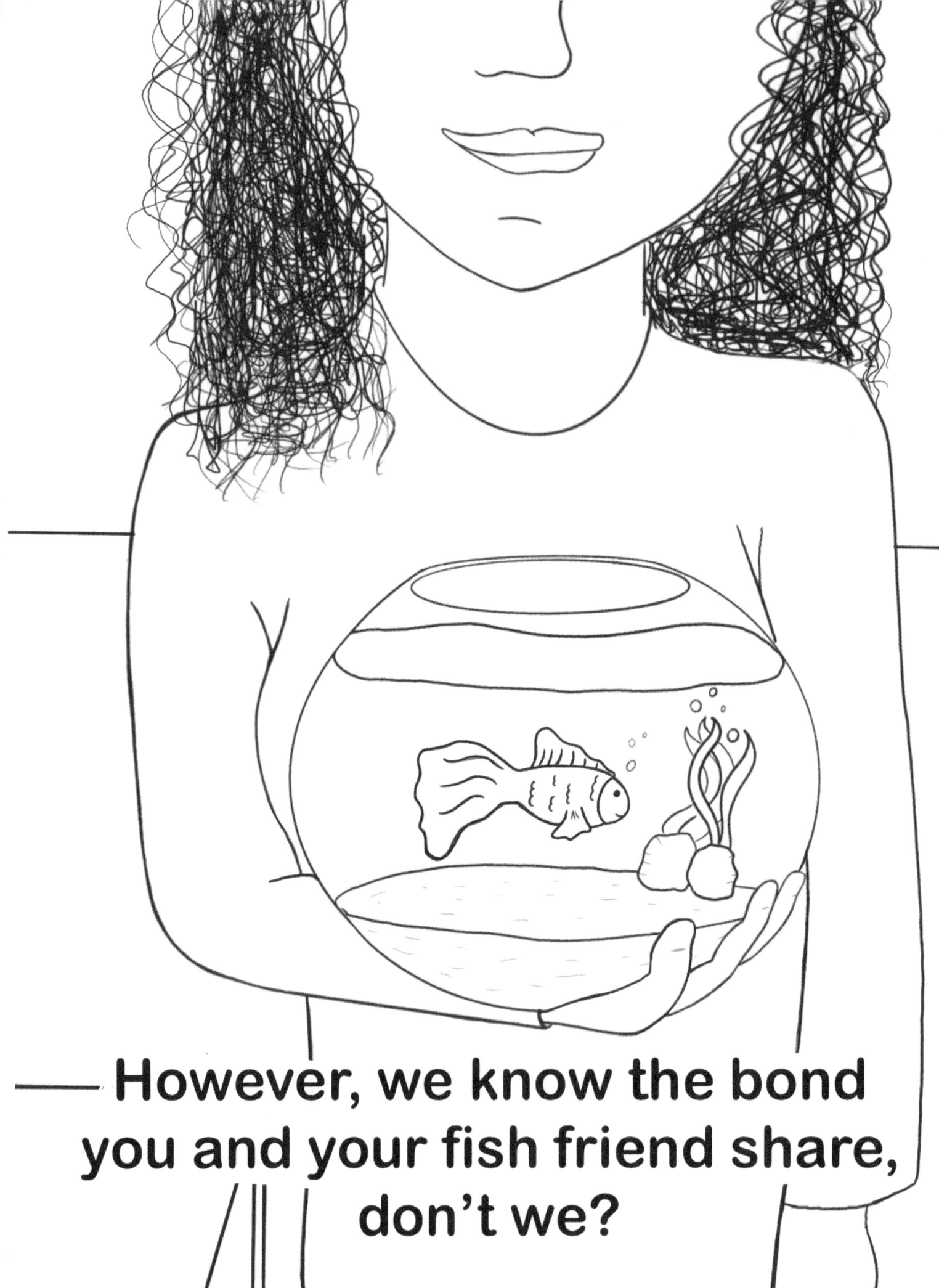

However, we know the bond you and your fish friend share, don't we?

Your relationship has always been so special.

The happiness shared between you and your friend has been contagious to see.

We understand how difficult it may be to not see your little finned friend everyday.

We also know there is little we can say to help ease the discomfort at this time.

Just be aware you are so loved, and we are so proud of you for how you've matured while having a pet.

Having a pet isn't always glamorous and fun, sometimes it's real work.

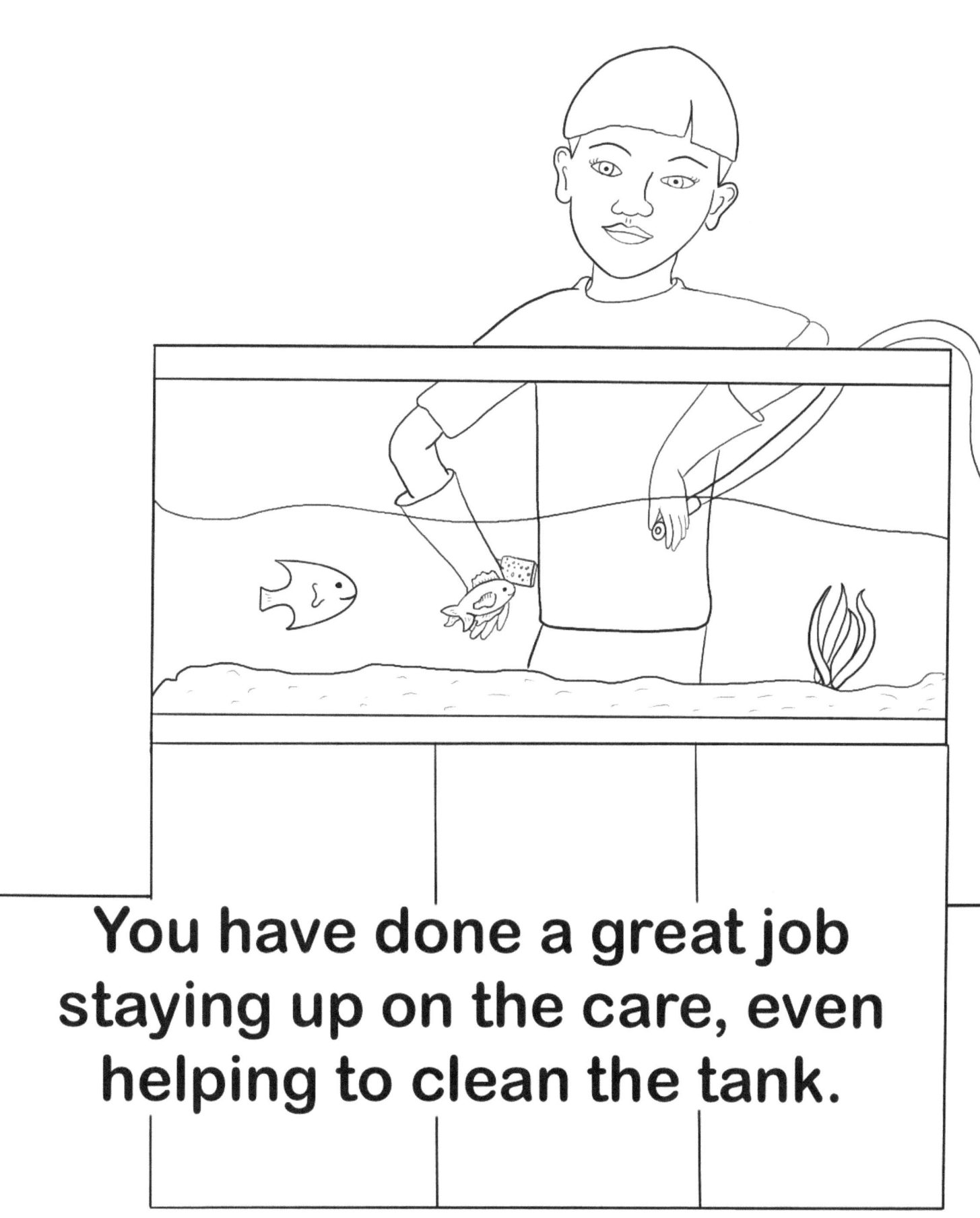

You have done a great job staying up on the care, even helping to clean the tank.

If you get sad you can always think back on the great memories you've made together.

Like how excited you felt when you received your finned friend.

Or how if you would put your finger on the tank, your companion would follow it around.

For now these memories may bring tears to your eyes, but know with time your tears will subside.

Then when you think back fondly on your amazing finned friend, you will smile and be so grateful for what time you had together.

You always have support here for you if you wish to talk about anything.

Whether we sit crying, or laughing, about memories together, we will get through this as a team.

Never forget you are loved
forever and always.
Love, _____

Friend's Facts

Friend's Name:_____

Friend's Age:_____

Friend's Favorite Food/s:_____

_____

Friend's Favorite Activity:_____

_____

Friend's Favorite Toy/s: _____

_____

Friend's Favorite Person/s:_____

_____

Feel free to write a little note, or share a memory or two.

Sorry To Hear About Your Fish, is one of the books in the children's line from Colleen's Bereavement Line For Children. Colleen's Bereavement Line for Children is aimed to assist in the healing process of children that find themselves navigating the loss of a loved one or pet. Sorry To Hear About Your Fish focuses specifically on those with a fish friend. A name can be added to the beginning of the book, while in the back of the book there is space to write memories about the scaly friend. Followed by a page for "Friend Facts" that can be filled in for a more personal feel.

All animal books in the series are interactive as well, they are in a coloring book format. Art has been shown as a useful tool that can aid in the healing process.